MODERN PARABLES

A Collection of Short Stories

WRITTEN BY Richa and Alex Sonifrank

Modern Parables: A Collection of Short Stories

DEDICATED TO
OUR DAUGHTER,
SITA

Table of Contents

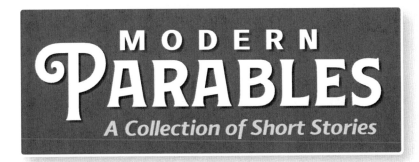

WRITTEN BY Richa and Alex Sonifrank

The King's Festivals

Mark was young when he became king. He wanted to celebrate his new status and threw one of the greatest autumn festivals that the world had ever seen. He took all the traditions and ceremonies he had grown up with and made them as large and exciting as possible.

Each year, he held the same festival and tried to make it larger and more exciting than the year before, always maintaining the traditions of his youth.

King Mark was incredibly happy, but as the years passed, he grew frustrated. People started wearing different clothing than what was popular when Mark was young. They started to celebrate with different foods and drinks than anything Mark grew up enjoying. The youngest started celebrating with traditions that were not like the traditions he remembered.

Eventually, his autumn festival became unrecognizable to him. Mark grew older and had kids and grandkids and saw his own grandchildren celebrating the coming of autumn in ways he had never seen.

King Mark's dissatisfaction grew so much, he decided to make a decree. The autumn festival would return to the exact same celebration it had been when he first became king. He would show the youngest how great the old ways were and force them to maintain those traditions to ensure the autumn festival would never change.

Invitations were sent out and King Mark specifically requested the presence of the great sage of the mountains. The town respected him and his wisdom as he was the oldest person in the kingdom. No one knew just how old he was. Mark believed that once the sage witnessed the festival and spoke of the greatness of the traditions, the rest of the kingdom would understand.

Fewer people came to this festival, and among the youngest, it was clear they were not enjoying themselves. Among those that did still attend was the great sage who had traveled down from the mountains.

King Mark greeted this respected elder but was surprised to be met with hostility.

"What's this strange clothing everyone is wearing?" shouted the sage. "It looks nothing like how people dressed when your father held the autumn festival."

King Mark fumbled his words.

"And what's this unusual food everyone is eating? Where are all the traditional dishes like your grandfather used to have at his autumn festival?"

King Mark remained silent; he was unsure how to respond.

"Where are the twirling towers, and the rock tosses, and all the traditions that your great-grandfather used to have at the autumn festival? This festival has no respect for tradition."

King Mark approached the wise sage. "I believe I understand the point," he said.

The sage looked around and smiled. "Good thing, actually. All those old traditions had gotten stale. I can't wait to see what's new next year."

From that year onwards, King Mark let the people celebrate as they wished. Every year things changed, but King Mark always saw joy from the people celebrating.

No tradition is permanent.
Best to celebrate the change.

Sold Out

Two brothers both loved candy. Fortunately for them, their uncle Frank was a respected candy maker in the town. Frank made candy in his factory which was sold at candy stores all around the city.

Uncle Frank had just released a new candy that he was sure his nephews would love.

When the two brothers heard the news, they ran to their local shop to buy the new candy. Unfortunately when they arrived, their uncle's new candy had sold out. While the first brother was disappointed, the second realized it meant his uncle was doing well for himself. The second brother was happy for his uncle.

A bad outcome from one perspective
can be a good outcome from another perspective.

ᏢREACHING

One day, Tom was having lunch with friends and noticed Sally had brought her own bottle along with metal cutlery to the restaurant. It seemed very peculiar, so Tom asked about it.

"Oh, I'm just trying to cut down on waste," said Sally humbly.

Tom had never really thought of how many plastic cups and forks he had thrown out over the years. He always liked to think he did his best for the environment.

"Good for you, but you don't have to be so preachy about it," Tom blurted out.

As Tom left, he recognized Sally was putting in extra effort and he didn't like realizing he wasn't doing his best.

Do not scorn a message
because it resonated with you.

THE DIRTY RIVER

Sue and Tom walked to school together most mornings and talked each day along the way. Tom was deeply knowledgeable about the world at large and often complained about its problems.

On the way to school, they walked along a small river. One day, the two of them noticed trash in the river. They could see it had come from materials in the student's lunches. It polluted the river and looked ugly. They both saw animals caught up in the trash and were sad about this.

"We should do something," said Sue.

"This is bad, but compared to rivers being polluted in the West, this is not a big deal," said Tom.

That day, Sue and Tom were both frustrated. Sue didn't want to accept Tom's reasoning and decided it would be better to do something. The following day, she started talking to other students and trying to make sure everyone was more careful with how they disposed of their lunches.

Tom did see the progress. But instead of praising Sue, he complained, "Compared to the struggles of those to the South, why would you worry about this?"

Sue ignored the comment from Tom. Instead, she started working on collecting a little bit of the trash from the river each day on the way to school. At first, she was all by herself but soon other kids started to join in. Eventually teachers and even the principal lent a hand.

Tom witnessed all the progress Sue had made. Instead of being happy or supportive of his friend, Tom just felt frustrated.

Tom saw Sue trying very hard and could not understand why. He asked her, "Compared to everything else in the world, why focus on this?"

"Because it's something I can do," said Sue. "What have you done to make things better?"

*Thoughts and knowledge alone
don't lead to progress.*

Stress Relief

Jane and Lizy were old friends. They worked the same stressful job. One day they heard about goat therapy, which helps mitigate stress.

Lizy found a place that kept goats as therapy animals where people could pay to visit the goats and spend time with them. Lizy loved the experience and felt less stressed.

Jane knew a place that kept rescued goats that needed help. Jane volunteered to help the rescued goats. She had goats all around her the entire time. They would bump into her and they seemed to enjoy watching her work. She felt fulfilled having helped the sanctuary.

That Sunday, the two friends met, and Jane shared with Lizy her experience of feeling stress-free *and* rewarded. Lizy was glad to have stress relieved but felt Jane had made the better decision.

Doing good is inherently rewarding.

ᎢHE ᏁQUARIUM

The local aquarium was likely going to close. The idea of keeping dolphins or whales in captivity was not popular among kids, but many of the older residents of the town wanted the aquarium to stay open.

Many adults recognized the kids were in the right but still wanted to find a way to keep the aquarium open. The adults had many memories from when they were young and wanted to carry that on to the new generation. A group of politicians got together to figure out how to keep the town's aquarium in business. They put in a lot of time and effort to keep it open and had many ideas to present.

To the elders' frustration, the kids were uninterested in anything presented to them. Bigger stages, different food, new activities, not even one idea resonated with them. Each time a new idea was presented, the kids would just say, "That sounds neat, but I don't think any living being should be captured just for the sake of entertainment."

The older people in town could not accept this. They kept putting in more time and effort to make their plan succeed but nothing they did ever worked to keep the aquarium open.

If the younger generation has better ethics,
then it's better to embrace them.

THE MEAN DOGGIE

There was a little doggy named Spot. He often barked and lashed out at other dogs. He was very afraid of them.

Often, he would see a dog and jump to bark and bite at them but would fall off his chair and hurt himself.

The other dogs just wanted to play, but Spot was too scared. He kept hurting himself from his fear—which just made him more afraid.

If you nourish your fear,
it will grow.

Two Churches

Two churches stood across the street from each other. While many in the community enjoyed both, Carl was deeply passionate about his church.

This passion took a dark turn when he started to criticize members of the other church. Carl spoke loudly and with passion about how some did not dress well enough. He started to condemn specific members of the other church, talking about how they did not spend enough time with their families or that their kids were misbehaved.

He became more and more negative, and many people listened to him. He always claimed he spoke like this for the community's own good and that he wanted to make sure everyone in both churches acted well.

One day, Carl found out that Mark, a singer in his church's choir, had stolen from someone. Members of the church asked Carl about the situation, but he stayed silent. Police came to the church to arrest Mark. Some people in the church asked Carl to explain, but he stayed silent. Word got out in the town about what had happened, and many asked for Carl's opinion, but he had no comment.

The next week, Carl spoke of the poor hygiene of the other church, but now no one in his church cared to listen.

You need to recognize the fault within.

Ant Problems

Abdul tended to leave crumbs all over the house. He would eat while standing and walking around and was such a messy eater that food would always fall on the ground. He would forget to clean up after dinner and would leave food outside all the time.

One day, while Abdul was having his sandwich, he saw a few ants walking about on the counter. It was just a few, and he didn't think much of it, but a few days later, he found his place covered in ants.

Abdul panicked. He tried to sweep them all up to take them outside, and thought he had gotten them all, but the next morning he woke to find even more ants.

He went to the store to find solutions and bought all kinds of repellent. While some worked temporarily, he would eventually wake up to find more ants.

He decided to dedicate time to sealing up the house to keep them out. He went outside, patching cracks in his old house and covering the kitchen in sealant to keep out the little critters. After days of work, Abdul felt like he finally had fixed the issue.

The next day, he woke up and found gnats in his house. They were swarming the banana peels that were left out. At that point, Abdul realized the real problem was not the old house but how he cleaned up after himself.

Better to fix the problem at its source.

12

The Flawed Restaurant

Martin and Bob loved going to Street Deli for lunch. They enjoyed the food and the aesthetics of the restaurant.

On Monday, Martin and Bob went to Street Deli and had a great time. But when they were leaving, they saw the owner, Sal, yelling at and being mean to his kids.

On Tuesday, Martin and Bob went to Street Deli. They did not enjoy it as much as before. When they were leaving, they saw Sal screaming at a server and making him cry.

On Wednesday, Martin and Bob went to Street Deli. They still ordered but did not enjoy being there at all. When they were leaving, they saw Sal yelling at and throwing stones at a street dog.

On Thursday, Martin went to Street Deli alone and Bob went to Pat's Diner next door. Martin wished he had not seen Sal act that way while Bob enjoyed his time at Pat's Diner.

On Friday, Bob invited Martin to join him at Pat's Diner.

"But I love Street Deli! I've always gone there," said Martin.

Bob had a great time at Pat's Diner, while Martin continued to wish he had not seen Sal's bad behavior.

Do not regret new information.

THE WAITRESS

Rashi worked through college as a waitress at a restaurant. She was a horrible worker. She was sloppy, showed up late, and found every opportunity to slack off and dodge her duties. Despite this, she always felt she could run things better and hoped one day to have her own restaurant.

Years passed, and Rashi was delighted to find that she had acquired her uncle's restaurant. She quickly began to struggle with the staff.

Rashi believed the staff was slacking off and distrusted them. She observed them closely and never let people work independently. She assumed everyone was a bad worker and her vigilance was the only way to prevent it.

Rashi was exhausted working this way and kept losing staff members who could not tolerate her micromanagement. The restaurant never became successful.

If you are the type to cheat,
you will have a hard time trusting others.

SUNFLOWER SEEDS

One morning, Mrs. Laverne planted sunflower seeds all over her backyard.

Two birds came later that day and started digging up the sunflower seeds. One bird saw a beehive nearby and got upset, as they never liked having bees buzz around them.

The second bird turned to first and realized he was upset at the beehive. "We only have these seeds in the ground because last year the bees pollinated the flowers. You should try to be less bothered by their buzzing."

You may rely on
those different from you.

BEING NICE

John always worked hard and got along with everyone, so it was no surprise when he was promoted to supervisor.

After his promotion, Robert ended up working directly under John. Robert was not the best at his job. He made significant mistakes, some of which created a lot of extra work for his co-workers.

Despite this, John always tried to be nice to Robert. He wanted to be a nice supervisor and be on people's good side. He would tell Robert to keep at it and keep trying but never gave him harsh or constructive feedback that could help him improve. John and his team often had to work extra to pick up what Robert did wrong. Due to Robert's mistakes, he was put on probation.

Robert was sad letting people down but John could only speak kindly and act nice. John wanted Robert to feel good about himself and did not want Robert to dislike him.

Eventually, the other supervisors got together and decided to fire Robert. John felt like he had failed Robert and his other coworkers. He carried the guilt with him.

Sometimes being nice is not helpful.

THE TOWN FOREST

A town was built alongside a large forest. All the people, young and old, loved the forest. The kids loved to play games and pick berries in the forest, while the parents went on long walks that kept them healthy and happy. The oldest visited the forest to relive their memories and to teach kids about nature.

The town also relied on the forest for work, and each year they would harvest some of the trees to sell for lumber and to make new homes. Eventually, some in the town decided they wanted larger homes or more wooden items and that they needed to take more from the forest. As the forest was so large, this seemed like it would not be an issue.

Over time, the people of the town wanted more and more from the forest. The edge of the forest started to move back but so slowly that no one noticed. Each year, the difference was indistinguishable from the last, but one year, the townspeople went to collect from the forest and realized there was nothing left.

Greed will always catch up to you.

Two Students

Nigel and Nia were good students. Nigel could easily memorize everything for a test, but it took Nia much more time. Nia needed to better understand things to commit them to memory. Sometimes, Nigel would make fun of how long it took Nia to learn.

One day, the kids were out getting some chocolate. Somewhere, they must have taken a wrong turn because they ended up lost.

Nigel began to freak out. He did not really know what to do and could not think clearly. Nia tried to calm herself and reflected on everything she had learned.

Nia used the setting sun to determine which direction to start walking. They had both learned in school how the rising and setting of the sun occurred but only Nia was able to apply that knowledge to their situation. In no time at all, they arrived back home.

Being able to implement what you learned
is more important than learning more.

THE PUPPY

Brad loved visiting the family next door because they had a new dog. The puppy they adopted was full of energy. Brad would visit and run around with the puppy and have a lot of fun. He wanted his own puppy and decided to ask for one for his birthday.

Upon hearing Brad's request, his parents refused. Both of his parents often worked late and would be unavailable to give the dog the attention it needed. Worst of all, his parents did not believe he was responsible enough to take care of a dog. They told Brad he was too interested in going to the mall with his friends or playing video games late into the night. Brad screamed and shouted every mean thing he could think of, but his parents would not budge. They made it clear Brad was not getting a dog.

Not long after their argument, Brad found out the neighbors were taking a short vacation and needed a dog sitter. This time, Brad had a plan—he would show his parents how easy it was to care for a puppy, and they would change their mind. When Brad suggested they take the dog for a few days, the parents agreed, but only because it was temporary. His parents seemed to believe it would teach Brad a lesson.

The first day, Brad came home late because he decided to linger at school with his friends. When he got home, he realized the dog had made a mess of the entire house. When Brad's parents got home, they made Brad clean it up since the dog was meant to be his responsibility.

The second day, Brad got home early to take out the dog. He regretted not spending more time with his friends but did not want to have to clean up again. Instead, he stayed up late playing video games. The next day, the dog started whining and begging to go out and be fed much earlier than Brad wanted to get up. The day was rough on him.

The third day, Brad felt unhappy, and decided to go around town. But this time, he took the dog with him so he would not make a mess again. He thought he had finally solved the problem. But none of the shops or restaurants would let him in with the dog, and eventually, he had to go back home.

The fourth day, Brad eagerly gave back the dog. He was happy his parents had not listened to him when he previously demanded a dog.

You need to be ready for responsibilities
before you take them on.

ℬUSY ℱTUDENTS

ary and Sue attended the same school. They rode the bus together and lived close to one another.

On Monday, their friend Janette asked them to play after school. Mary and Sue both had assignments due, but Mary decided to play. Sue decided to go home and complete her schoolwork.

On Tuesday, Mary got in trouble for not finishing her work.

"Stupid Janette," thought Mary. "Why did she waste my time and invite me to play?"

On Wednesday, the theater was having a special showing of a popular film. Mary decided to go, but Sue decided to stay home and study for a quiz that they were going to have on Thursday.

Mary did poorly on her test, and as she looked at her score, she cursed the theater for having a special the day before her test.

When it came time for final grades, Mary performed poorly and was very frustrated.

"Why did I have such a harsh teacher?" Mary said. "They are so mean to give me a bad grade."

Sue looked at her high grade and turned to Mary. "I don't think you have the teacher to blame," she said.

Recognize when you are the problem.

FUTURE PROBLEMS

One day, Darryl ran out of toothpaste. *I guess I'll just skip today. One day won't hurt,* he thought. Darryl skipped brushing his teeth that day, and the next day he did not really notice a difference.

Darryl got terribly busy that week and never found time to buy toothpaste. After one week, he still did not notice any difference.

Darryl kept putting it off because every day, it did not seem like things were any worse than the day before.

One day, Darryl saw a picture taken many years earlier. He realized his gums were unhealthy and that his teeth had yellowed over time. He went to the dentist the next day and discovered he had many cavities.

You eventually pay for your mistakes.

THE THREE SONS

Jim was a proud father of three boys. He taught them well to ensure they were smart, confident, and capable men. Jim was well-respected in the community for maintaining the town's most popular religious center.

The center provided many services for the community. It helped people without a home by giving them shelter and food so they could find new work. It ran a program for people recovering from addiction. It also served as a place for older people to meet up and swap stories. The center helped a lot of people every year, and Jim was proud of it.

As Jim grew older, he began thinking about the center's future. He hoped he had raised his sons to continue its legacy. On his final days, Jim gathered his sons together to ask them to look after this piece of their community that he had lovingly built. Jim passed away shortly thereafter, leaving his sons to take charge.

The first son was content with things as they were. He did his best to maintain the programs that existed and kept them going strong. He was not interested in improving the center, but he made sure everything worked as it always had.

The second son was excited to explore ways that the center could become the greatest asset to his community. He researched new plans and methods for people in recovery to ensure they were successful. He studied how best to help homeless people in the community find work and best take advantage of programs available to them. He even found ways to help the elderly use technology to connect with their kids while they were visiting. He looked at this progress and was extremely proud and satisfied with his work.

The third son heard of a new religious center coming up in the area. He went to visit. He saw a giant structure bigger than anything else in town. Inside, he saw passionate speakers. The new center had a bookstore as well as a vitamin shop. After service, they sold meals made in an onsite kitchen. Everything was very pristine and glamorous.

The third son struggled after this visit. He came up with a plan to eliminate the program that helped the homeless people, and instead dedicated that space to more exciting options. He wanted to make more money to expand his father's center and make it larger. He wanted to charge the elderly that used the space during the day as he was sure they had a lot of money.

The third son got to work quickly on his plan, but immediately was blocked by his brothers. They brought a photo book of their late father that showcased all the hard work Jim had put into the programs as well as the pride he had in them. The third son realized he may have corrupted the meaning of his father's last wish.

Find the true meaning within the words.

LATE HOMEWORK

Both Jared and Molly neglected to do their homework and therefore, had to do their homework on their lunch break.

Jared was very frustrated that he couldn't spend time with his friends. On the other hand, Molly respected that she had made a mistake and accepted her punishment. Her acceptance helped her feel content about the situation.

Seek to accept your mistakes.

BEST FRIENDS

Terry and Ashley always had lunch together at school. They called each other best friends.

Ashley was a bit hot tempered and got into a big argument with another girl in the class, Melissa. Ashley knew that her best friend Terry was also friends with Melissa and decided that Terry needed to pick a side.

"I don't want you to talk to Melissa anymore," Ashley said to Terry. "She is no good and if you keep hanging out with her, we won't be friends anymore."

Terry didn't respect such a rule and let Ashley know as much.

Time passed and Terry and Ashley had stopped having lunch together. Ashley also started having a very hard time in her math class. She used to work together with Terry to help understand the class better.

Terry still cared for her friend and knew that Melissa was the best in school at math. Terry decided to ask Melissa to help Ashley.

One day Melissa saw Ashley struggling to complete her math assignment. Melissa offered to help. Ashley hesitated but decided to accept. Melissa was very kind and helped make sure Ashley understood everything.

"What made you decide to help me?" Ashley asked.

"Terry actually suggested I help you," Melissa said.

Ashley realized her mistake. The next day she apologized to Terry and Melissa both. From that day on, the three of them always had lunch together.

You shouldn't expect others to choose sides.

ᎢHE ᎯNXIOUS ᏢARENT

Sue and John had two young children. When their children were going to school, they got less exercise and education related to nutrition and physical health was limited. Sue decided to join the schoolboard, research how to best teach children about nutrition, and create materials for parents and teachers.

Meanwhile, John kept hearing the news about how the school system was lacking in terms of health teaching. He was constantly worried about his children, but instead of taking action, he only complained and felt anxious.

Sue explained to her kids about healthy living and, at the same time, helped other parents and felt fulfilled. She hoped that one day the situation would change so that every kid would be educated about healthy living and the school would improve and provide more opportunities for kids to exercise.

Action can help alleviate anxiety.

THE COUNTY FAIR

Carl, Tom, and Sue were close friends who loved going to the county fair. It was an event they looked forward to each year. They loved everything about it.

They all had many good memories and were looking forward to the next fair. Ahead of the next event, they read how the fair's owners had changed the policy in a way that would take more money from the shop owners—making it harder for those people to break even on the event.

Many shop owners had to drop out, and many others protested that the change had come too soon before the launch of the fair. It seemed there was a lot of conflict between the shop owners and the main organizer. It seemed like the fair this year would be quite different.

"The fair means a lot more to me than just the shops. I have so many memories there and even if the management is bad, it means something more to me," said Carl.

"I'm just going to skip this year. Hopefully, they fix it next year, but if they do not, I will find something else to do," said Sue.

Tom also felt attached to the event, but also wanted to skip it in solidarity with the shop owners. He summarized their complaints and wrote a story for the local paper. He contacted the county fair organizer to express their frustration and tried to get the word out to other people as well.

During this time, Carl was very frustrated. It seemed he was going to the fair alone this year. He went on opening day and tried his best to enjoy himself.

These friends did not live in a large town. Carl often encountered people that were impacted negatively by the change at the fair, and it made him feel uncomfortable. It made him wonder if he had done the right thing.

Sue found something else to do during the fair season. She enjoyed herself and happily went about her life.

Tom got to know many people in the area and was motivated to work with them to fix issues at the fair. He never felt he missed the fair.

After a year, the fair's owner gave in to pressure and made the changes requested by the shop owners. That year, all three friends went back to the fair together. Tom and Sue both felt good knowing they had not been a part of the fair the previous year.

*Not taking part in something negative
and working to try to fix it can both be valid options.*

ᴛʜᴇ ɴᴀɪʟ

One day, Mary was driving when the low tire pressure alert lit up on her car's dashboard panel.

Mary saw the alert but ignored it. Later that day, she noticed a nail in her tire. She told herself she'd address it tomorrow.

The next morning, Mary had plans to see her friends. Her friends were out having fun and Mary desperately wanted to join them. She thought of her tire but decided to put off fixing it because she was running late.

On her way to join her friends, Mary heard a loud "pop," and realized her tire had completely burst. Mary had to call a towing company.

She waited for the tow truck to arrive and got a ride to the repair shop. When she got there, she was billed for the towing, a brand-new tire, and for replacing the metal rim on the tire. By the time everything was fixed, it was also late.

As she waited in line to pay, someone in front of her was paying for their patched tire. The person's tire had a simple nail in it and patching it had been a quick and inexpensive fix.

Better to fix problems right away before they get worse.

Net Positive

Ram and Jack were good friends. They both wanted to help people when they grew up. As they got older, they acted on their goals.

It took Ram a long time to sit down and come up with how he could help the community. His focus was to help—but also, he wanted to minimize harm along the way. He decided to dedicate his life to growing vegetables. He hired many people from the community. He also did a lot of research to determine what would do well in that area to minimize waste and ensure everything grew well.

On the other hand, Jack decided to run a cattle ranch. He raised cows and slaughtered them for food. He hired many people from his community and provided them with jobs. He also donated food to his community. However, the people who worked at his ranch were traumatized by their jobs; it caused some of them anxiety because they were around violence. Families did not take their kids to the ranch because they knew the kids would be sad knowing the animals were to be killed.

Jack decided to visit Ram one day to see how he was doing on their combined goal. He saw the vast amount of food Ram was able to grow. Jack realized his heart was in the right place, but he had made the situation worse not better. From there, Jack decided to commit to learning from Ram to help feed the town.

Ensure your actions
produce a net positive.

Finding the Right Way

Ben and Craig enjoyed going to their local market to buy chicken. They loved eating it.

One day, they decided to visit the farm they always bought from because they thought it would be fun to see where their favorite food comes from. What they saw horrified them.

The chickens lived in poor conditions. Their beaks were missing and some of them didn't have any feathers. They were oversized and some couldn't even move.

Ben decided to stop buying chicken. What he saw was too much for him.

Craig decided to stop supporting that farm, but he didn't want to give up his favorite food. He found another farm and decided that would work. He was worried, so he visited and found the chickens treated in much the same way as the first farm.

Craig was still determined to hold onto his favorite food. He found many farms far away he thought would be good, but each time he visited, they were just as bad as before.

Eventually, Craig decided to give up on chicken as well. He had tried hard to find something better and ultimately wished he had followed Ben's example from the beginning.

Sometimes we have to give up things
we love to do the right thing.

The Pig

Charlie was a happy-go-lucky potbelly pig living with others in a junkyard. He never stopped to wonder why they lived there and instead spent his time rooting around and trying to find something to eat.

Charlie was born in the peak of summer, and when the first winter came around, he had a hard time. He was chilly every day and could not find any food in the cold ground. The human who was supposed to feed them did not often come.

Many of Charlie's family seemed to get sick and weak. Eventually, an illness came to Charlie and after a difficult time, he managed to fight it off.

One day, a whole bunch of humans showed up and started to round up all the pigs. They caught some of Charlie's friends and put them in crates. Charlie hated these people and tried his best to run from them, but eventually they caught him.

Charlie was very scared while the truck was taking him away. Eventually, they took him off the truck and put him in a big space with many other pigs. They were all running around and seemed happy.

Charlie was very scared at first, but eventually came to love it in his new home. The place had a big barn that stayed warm all year, there was always lots of food, and he never got sick. The people were nice, and he can do whatever his pig brain wanted to do. Even though he fought it at first, he was glad that the people managed to move him to this new place.

Positive change can be hard
but will always be worthwhile.

The Bad Boss

William worked many nights and weekends for several years to make sure the company he worked for did well. After all his hard work, he was promoted to one of the top positions at his job.

After William had worked so hard for the new position, he began to worry that others in the company would try to undermine him to help themselves move up in the company. William feared some of these people would make up bad stories about him or try to take credit for work he had done. To keep himself safe, William made sure he got all the credit for successes in the company and passed all the blame to others when things went poorly.

William became more and more difficult to work with and more projects he was involved with began to fail. He became more and more stressed with time to ensure he kept performing well but could never let go of this paranoia of his coworkers. The job began to impact William's health.

Being paranoid about others
will only cause harm to yourself.

A New Farmer

Mark acquired a piece of land and was eager to become a farmer just like his father and grandfather before him.

Mark got to work just how he farmed with his father and his grandfather. In those days, the work seemed quite easy. They put down seeds and mulch and things grew naturally every year.

Mark wanted farming to be as easy as he remembered, but he kept encountering problems. Sometimes it rained too much, and the soil washed away. Sometimes it didn't rain at all, and the plants withered. Weeds came up abundantly and crops suffered.

Mark returned to his father's farm for advice. He said, "Dad, I don't understand. It was always so easy every year growing up."

His father replied, "Mark, you weren't around at the beginning. We had troubles. Sometimes it rained too much, and the soil washed away, and sometimes it didn't rain enough, and the plants withered. We had weeds choking the crops."

Mark listened in disbelief. He had no idea of such challenges.

"Luckily, your grandfather helped me get through it. We worked extra hard that next year to lay down better mulch and remove the weeds. We studied what plants worked well together and stayed up every night reading. We built ways to ensure water got to the crops and the soil held the moisture. That year, we worked harder than we had ever worked. The following year, we worked hard, but didn't need to do quite as much. After a while, we just needed to put down new mulch and seeds."

With that, Mark set to work. He worked harder than ever that next year, but each year after that he needed to do less and less.

⇒———·———⇐

Building a good foundation
can make things easier later.

The Broken Truck

Steve was driving his new Ford truck to work. All of a sudden, it started making an odd noise and he had to pull off to the side of the road.

"Let me lend a hand," offered a man driving past in a car.

"How could you help?" said Steve. "You drive a car and wouldn't understand how to fix a truck." With that, the man in the car drove off.

"Let me lend a hand," offered a woman driving past in a different brand of truck.

"How could you help?" said Steve. "You drive a different truck and wouldn't understand how to help with mine." With that, the woman drove off.

"Let me lend a hand," offered an old man driving an older model of the truck.

"How could you help?" said Steve. "You drive an older truck and wouldn't understand how to help with mine." With that, the old man drove off.

Just then, Steve saw a truck identical to his driving past, but the driver did not stop.

Help that comes from someone different
should be welcome.

THE HUNT

A long time ago, there was a kingdom that Dashrat one day would rule. Dashrat was a humble man and people from the kingdom could not wait for him to take the throne.

In the kingdom, the royals often hunted. Dashrat wanted to continue the tradition and traveled to the springs in the northern forest.

At the same time, Shrawan was traveling through the same forest. He was escorting his blind parents. As per his parent's wish, he was taking them on a pilgrimage. They stopped in the forest to collect water from the springs.

Dashrat often visited this forest but had never seen another person on his hunts. He heard noise coming from the springs and made a blind shot thinking it was a deer. Shrawan yelled in pain as the arrow pierced his chest. Dashrat rushed over and saw the dying Shrawan. With his dying breath, Shrawan asked Dashrat to fulfil his wish of giving water to his parents and asked him to take care of his parents.

Dashrat went to Shravan's parents to tell them what had happened. The shock of their son's death was too much for them, and, burdened by grief, they both died. With their dying breath they uttered a curse to Dashrat, that he would know the same suffering.

As years passed Dashrat painfully lived with the curse. He could feel one day the curse would manifest. As his sons grew up, fear was always in his mind.

When you plan to do harm,
you might end up hurting yourself.

THE YOUNG SAGE

Sunita was celebrated as the great sage of the town. Her teachings ensured the town stayed a successful and happy place.

Uma hoped to be the next town sage. She took up all the old texts and began frantically reading. She was jealous of the attention Sunita got, and hoped that the townspeople would listen to her instead.

Sunita heard Uma had been reading through many of the old texts vigorously and went to visit her. Uma had memorized many of the stories, but her interpretations were aggressive and hostile. Sunita heard this and suggested that Uma had much to grow before she could find value in the stories. Uma believed she was right and thought Sunita must not have studied properly.

Uma emerged from her studies with a message of aggression and violence. She gave impassioned lectures which sparked fear and anxiety in those who listened.

That year, many of the great sages were coming to visit the town. Uma believed they would witness how much she had learned and proclaim she was wise beyond her years. As they arrived, Uma began one of her impassioned sermons. The sages all listened.

After she was done, she approached them. To her surprise, they all looked quite disappointed.

"A broken vessel cannot hold water," one of them began. "You must mend yourself before you can find the value in the stories."

Having a pure mind must come before interpreting.

THE FANCY COAT

Katie loved her many fur coats—and loved to show them off to people. As years passed, many people became less excited to see them, and worse, many criticized her for wearing such clothes. They said the clothes came from bad practices, which made Katie very mad.

Katie went to the fur store she always visited to explain her situation. The store owner told her that the fur trade employed many people.

That day, Katie went back to her friends and tried to flaunt what she had learned. They all looked at her with frustration.

"Katie, any coat you would buy would support jobs. It is better to support the jobs that aren't cruel," said one of her friends. They pulled up articles and interviews with the people impacted by the fur trade. The evidence was too much, and Katie had to yield.

Katie went back to the fur store and the owner gave her another excuse for why their furs were good. This time, Katie was skeptical and decided to do her own investigation, only to find out the owner had once again lied to her. With regret, Katie decided to give up her fancy hobby.

A corrupt mind will always find
an excuse to do what they want.

SALLY'S RANCH

Sally always wanted to have a horse ranch where she could teach kids how to ride horses. It was a dream of hers since she was young.

After many years, Sally had finally saved up enough to launch her own horse camp. One of her friends suggested she wait until she learned more about it and that she should work at an existing ranch first. Sally refused; it was her dream to run the horse ranch, and she was eager to finally do that. She went to work right away buying the horses and buying the land for her ranch.

The first week at the ranch, Sally went to see her horses and realized they were all missing. The fencing she had built was not tall enough for the horses and they had all escaped and were running wild through the neighbors' backyards. Some of the horses even hurt themselves on the neighbors' fences. Many of the neighbors called the police because there were loose horses near their homes. It made Sally upset that the neighbors would do that to her.

The second week, she noticed many of the horses had sores on their mouths and were not eating much. She kept trying to feed them more hay, but they did not want it. Some of the neighbors again saw the horses in bad shape and called the police. It made Sally upset that the neighbors would do that. She was already having enough trouble. "Why are they so mean to me?" she would say.

It turned out the horses had gotten ill from a bad batch of hay. Sally did not know how to recognize it had gone bad and had to get all new hay for the horses. The neighbors looked at her with such anger. She would say to herself, "I'm the victim here! Why are they being so mean to me?"

The third week brought cold weather and snow. She came to see the horses and they were all struggling from the cold weather. Sally had not realized she needed to build them shelter and had not expected a cold front so early in the season. Their bad eating the previous week also did not help.

Sally was terribly upset seeing the horses in poor shape. But as soon as she managed to collect her thoughts, she saw the police at her door again. This time, they were not going to just leave. The police had come to take away her horses. She tried to explain but they would not listen to her. Couldn't they see she was the true victim here?

Her horses were moved away, and Sally's dreams were shattered. She decided to fight to get back her horses. It took some time, but she eventually discovered they were at a nearby horse rescue and went to confront the people who had her animals.

She arrived and saw her horses running happily in the field. They were healthier and stronger than she ever had seen them before. They seemed to love their new home.

Sally dropped to her knees. At that moment she realized they had been the victims all along.

Don't make yourself the victim;
understand your own responsibility
in any situation.

THE TEAM

Tim organized a local soccer team. The team often lost and had not done well in several years. Tim was frustrated at how poorly his team was performing but thought that he was incredibly good at soccer even though the league they played in was just for fun. Tim hoped for more good players to join him.

One day, Billy visited Tim's team and asked if he could join. Billy was athletic but never played soccer. He liked watching it on TV but did not really know how to play on a team.

"I shouldn't have to teach you!" shouted Tim. "We already have it bad enough not needing to waste time teaching you how to play. If you want to join, come back when you know how the game works."

Billy joined another team and trained with them. Eventually, he became good friends with his other teammates and never wanted to leave.

That season, Tim faced off against Billy's team. Yet again, Tim was defeated badly. After his loss, Tim wished he had better players, like Billy, on his team.

It is often your job
to help make people better.

THE CARING FATHER

Pandav was a great king, loved by many, and his sudden death shocked the kingdom. Upon his death, his brother Ditrash took the throne.

Ditrash was already quite old and needed to recognize an heir. Both Pandav and Ditrash had many children, and as the offspring got older, one became the clear best choice to become the king. Pandav's eldest child, Yid, was kind, knowledgeable, and wise beyond his years. The people all loved him dearly and all of Yid's siblings recognized his talent and were eager to support him as king. Ditrash recognized Yid as the best choice for the people, but Ditrash deeply loved his son, Durriyo.

Durriyo did not see yielding the throne to Yid as an option. He wanted to be in charge and was not willing to hear otherwise. For years, he demanded his father pass him the throne. Durriyo was talented but could not connect and serve the kingdom.

As the children came of age, Ditrash understood the right course of action was to retire and pass the kingdom to Yid, but he struggled with the cries and demands of his prized son, Durriyo. Ditrash cursed his fate—he had lost his brother and inherited the throne only to later be challenged on how best to relinquish it. He wanted to give to his son what the child wanted and feared the outcome if Durriyo did not get what he wanted.

Ditrash went to Durriyo to discuss the transfer of the kingdom. Ditrash explained that Yid was recognized by the people as the rightful king and that Yid was the most qualified for the role. Upon hearing this, Durriyo lashed out. He became sad beyond reason, and angry without end. Ditrash hated seeing his child in such anguish.

Ditrash went to Yid to discuss and express his worries. Yid knew Ditrash was not on the right path, but that avoiding conflict was best for the people. He suggested the kingdom be divided in a way to give Durriyo the largest portion. Yid hoped this would satisfy Durriyo's desires. The plan seemed agreeable to Ditrash.

Durriyo heard of this plan and was enraged. Having most of the kingdom was not enough. Durriyo immediately started rallying soldiers and weapons to fight Yid.

Yid saw the incoming battle and expertly assembled his soldiers. Yid's cunning and talent allowed him to easily outmaneuver Durriyo and quickly defeat him. During the battle, Durriyo was fatally wounded and, in his final moments, cursed his fate.

With three conflicts resolved, Yid took control of the kingdom and spent his years as a wise king that brought prosperity to the kingdom. Ditrash spent the remainder of his years mourning his son.

If you do wrong for your loved one,
you both will end up paying the consequences.

CRADUATION

The Smith family and the Jones family were happy to greet each other on graduation day. Each family saw their youngest child graduate. The families were neighbors, and the kids had grown up together.

Each family was excited to see their child graduate, but the Smith family had a somber note to their celebration. The parents were unsure what to do with their life now. Everything had been dedicated to their children. Their life revolved around soccer practice and weekend tournaments. They organized elaborate birthday parties and playdates all year round. Each day, they looked forward to planning the next big thing for their kids.

The Jones parents always made time for their kids, and ensured they were well-raised but still found time to do good. They planned their life around helping others and would often take the kids as well. They volunteered at the dog adoption center nearby and the kids had great fun walking the older dogs. They organized food drives and the kids were excited to make sandwiches. The parents loved gardening and the kids were always amazed seeing these little plants turn into food.

Ultimately, all the kids loved their lives and their childhood. The Smith family was proud that they did a good job raising their kids, but just had no idea how to live their lives now. The Jones family were excited for their kids and had no worries about what came next.

Don't rely on someone else
to give your life meaning.

Two Farmers

Santosh and Anil were farmers in a small village. Santosh was well-respected as one of the village's elders. He always worked hard, and his farm did very well. When he grew extra, he always gave it back to the community to help farmers who did not do well that year. He helped the younger farmers get started and taught them how to succeed. Many people came to him with problems, and he helped resolve them.

Anil was jealous of Santosh. Anil wanted to be respected like this.

One day, a wise sage passed through the village on a pilgrimage. Everyone in town came to see the sage and hear his teachings. Anil saw how the village treated the sage and decided he wanted that respect for himself.

Anil decided to follow the sage for some time as a disciple. He began to dress like the sage and memorized many of the

49

parables of the sage. He memorized all of the sage's rituals and practices.

In some time, Anil returned to the village and continued to act as he had learned from the sage. To his frustration, the village still looked to Santosh for advice.

A year later, the sage returned to the village. He watched the townspeople and saw Santosh working hard to help the village.

Anil greeted the sage. "Master, I have followed everything you have taught me. Why is Santosh still the one respected?"

The sage replied, "I have never seen someone that follows the old teaching so well. Why would you follow me when there is someone like this in the town?"

Do not focus on the superficial aspects of teaching.

The Bank Robber

Robert thought he was a smart guy. He also thought he could use some extra cash. He'd been keeping an eye on a bank for a while and realized when the guards tended to go out for lunch. He thought with the right timing he'd be able to stage a robbery and get away with some extra cash.

Robert thought he'd be able to steal just enough for a nice vacation and a break from work. Maybe he'd get a nicer TV. He figured it'd be a one time thing for a little boost to his own wallet.

He planned everything perfectly and when the day arrived, everything went smoothly. Robert found himself with a nice sack of cash and was happy. He took some time off work and enjoyed his success.

The money didn't last forever and soon Robert found himself back at his job, working to pay bills. He hated every day of it. He remembered how easy it was to rob the bank.

It had worked before, so Robert ran through things just like last time. This time though, the bank had adjusted things and Robert was caught in the act.

Once you let yourself do something wrong,
it's harder to resist the temptation to do it again.

RICOCHET

Wyatt and Bill loved firing off their air rifles. They took turns and boasted about their aim.

One day, Wyatt picked up the rifle to head into the woods and shoot at tin cans as they always did.

"I'm tired of shooting cans," said Bill. "Let's head down by the road and shoot at signs."

Wyatt did not think that was a good idea, but Bill was persistent. "If anyone drives by, that's just the universe putting them there. It's not our responsibility what happens."

The two of them went and shot up signs until a bullet ricocheted off and hit a passing car. The driver got out of his car, and while very irate, grabbed the air rifle and broke it over his knee.

Taking negative action isn't leaving it to the universe.

TRASH DAY

Sam used to rely on the trash service coming twice a week. He had a big family, and they produced a lot of food scraps.

One day, the trash service announced they were changing to once-a-week pickups. This meant that trash ended up sitting in Sam's house and it got very smelly. Sometimes, his house produced more than could fit in the bin and he had to pile bags up outside. If those bags broke while sitting outside, Sam needed to get on his knees and pick up all of the smelly garbage.

Sam started to hear about efforts to minimize waste. This could help reduce unnecessary waste and help people at large, but most important for Sam, it could help solve his trash problem.

First, Sam investigated composting. It took some time to understand and the first week he did it, things were somewhat hard. The house was in the habit of throwing things out, and it was challenging to remember to put things into a compost bin. They eventually started using a bin in the freezer to store food scraps for a bit, and then would take them out over time. It was still quite different, but after a few weeks the family got into the rhythm of things.

One day, Sam realized it did not take any effort to compost. He produced good fertilizer for his garden and did not really have to try at all.

Eventually, Sam wondered if he could do more. He kept adding and tweaking new ways to do more and, over time, they became part of his routine and second nature. One week, Sam went to put out the trash for pickup and realized he did not even have one bag for collection.

Change takes effort at first,
but quickly becomes easy.

THE BRIGHT KID

Diya was a very bright kid. At school, everything came easily and she rarely needed to pay attention in class.

One day, Diya's dad took her outside to teach her about different poison plants. He talked about poison ivy and poison oak and showed her many examples. Through his explanation,

Diya thought about her cats and the next book she wanted to read. She did not really pay any attention to her dad.

The next year, Diya was playing outside and running through the woods. Later that day, she realized she had come down with a terrible rash over her whole body.

Diya's dad took her back outside the next day to teach her how to identify poison ivy and this time she gave him her complete focus.

---

*Better to learn
before you face consequences.*

THE MAYOR

Lee had big ideas about who he was going to be, with a lot of ideas about how to make his state better and how to fix all the problems it faced. He was convinced he knew best and that everyone else should listen to him.

He decided to run for mayor of his town. He had a lot of energy and enthusiasm, and the people ultimately voted him into office.

Lee felt his ideas were bigger than what he could do as mayor. He never focused on the town but instead always spoke about how he could help everyone in the state.

Lee felt he was too good for his position as mayor and decided not to run again. Instead, he set his sights on becoming governor. He put all his efforts into his governor campaign and did not focus on his duties as mayor. After all, being mayor of that small town was beneath him because he had much grander ideas.

Voting day came and Lee eagerly awaited the results. He was shocked to see he had lost and worst of all, his little town had voted against him and ensured his defeat as mayor as well.

*Fulfill your obligations
before trying to take on bigger responsibility.*

THE SMART SOLUTION

Peggy grew up as the smartest kid in her school. She went to a good college and got a good job. At work, she always got the best projects and always was the smartest person on her team.

Peggy had two rowdy dogs and a quiet cat at home. She always had trouble keeping the two dogs out of the storage room. That was where she kept the dog and cat food, and it was also where she put the cat's litter box.

Peggy did not want to close the door to the room, as the cat needed to come and go throughout the day. She tried putting up pet gates, and tried training the dogs to stay out, but nothing worked. Eventually, Peggy gave up on fixing the problem and as she was so smart, she assumed no solution existed as she had not figured one out herself.

One day, Peggy's friend Scott was visiting and learned about the problem. Scott was a simple-minded person and Peggy wanted to vent to him about her problem.

"Why don't you just cut a hole in the door that's big enough for the cats, but too small for the dogs to fit through," Scott suggested.

It seemed so simple an idea, yet through all her attempts to come up with a solution, Peggy had never arrived at it. They got to work making a hole and the dogs could no longer get into the room.

*Sometimes a different set of eyes
can make a solution more obvious—
regardless of effort or talent.*

CHARITY EVENT

There was a beautiful city where the people lived a prosperous life. The people had nice houses, plenty of food, and were in good health.

While they were doing well, there was a small town just outside the city which was not so fortunate. The people there lived in run-down houses, they couldn't afford many things, and many of the kids had developed asthma.

Hearing about the kids with asthma troubled those in the city. Some of the members of the city decided to organize a charity event to buy inhalers for the kids. They wanted a charity event so they could raise money. After some deliberation, they organized a hot dog eating contest.

Many people attended the event and raised lots of money. At the end, the organizers had raised enough to buy all the kids inhalers. Everyone rejoiced, thinking how much good they had done.

The organizers wanted to go to town and meet the kids and give them the inhalers. When they got closer to the town, they started smelling the hot air. Even with closed windows, they started cough and wheeze.

Once the organizers finally arrived in the town, they realized the problem. There was a pig farm right across from many of the children's homes. The pigs were densely packed together and the filth was everywhere. The runoff from the pig waste ran everywhere. Seeing this, the organizers realized the actual problem and they learned a valuable lesson that day to resolve the cause instead of offering a bandage solution.

You are not doing a charitable act
by perpetuating the problem.

ᎬLECTION ᎠAY

There was a small country where many people did well but some of the poorest citizens struggled to eat.

Many of those better off in the country condemned the government and the politicians who had not solved this problem. Many protests were organized, and these people made it clear they wanted a solution. These people all viewed themselves as virtuous and kind and were frustrated that the government had not solved the problem.

Finally, a candidate came along that promised to solve the problem. The candidate put forth his plan to ensure every person in the country had access to food. The plan would turn many cotton fields into fields for crops and it would remove much of the meat production since much of the grain grown currently went to feed livestock.

The plan would easily ensure that no citizen would go hungry, but it would also mean the rest of the country would not be able to get as many new clothes. They would not be able to eat as much meat, but all the citizens would have food on their plate.

Election day came and the new candidate lost significantly. Most of the country hated the plan.

Sometime later people again began protesting and criticizing the government. They were very frustrated the government had still not ensured that no person would go hungry in their country.

Problems won't be solved
if you're unwilling to make changes to your life.

The Signs

Luke was an opinionated man. Luke was also a deeply angry man. He was angry at all the people around him and angry that they did not follow the same lifestyle as him. He believed he knew how to live correctly and hoped that everyone else would see the signs that he was right.

He was upset that some men did not eat in the manly way that he ate. He hoped they would get a sign of how wrong they were. Soon after, Luke started to have health problems.

Luke believed that men were too calm and needed to be more aggressive. Luke hoped they would get a sign of how wrong they were. Soon after, Luke began having issues with stress.

These problems continued to come to Luke, and he struggled more and more each day. But he continued to hope that everyone else would see the signs that he was right.

Be ready to see the signs yourself.

A FINAL THOUGHT

Eventually the greatest and richest man
will be thought of for the last time.

Everything physical is forgotten in time.

Aiding one person towards the right path
adds a positive energy to the universe
which lasts forever.

Every good deed is more permanent
than everything material.

DISCUSSION QUESTIONS

Which story do you connect to the most?

_____

What do you think when you think
of a words modern parables?

_____

_____

Are there any stories where you arrived
at different morals?

_____

_____

_____

Is there a lesson you feel is missing?

_____

_____

_____

Do you think the authors would include it?

_____

_____

_____

What was a story that you could not relate to
and do you think others would be able to relate?

_____

_____

_____

In the being nice story what John could have done differently and still be nice?

_____

_____

_____

From the net positive story, does any similar current issue comes to your mind?

_____

_____

_____

Where do you see people can gain from the moral Find the true meaning within the words?

_____

_____

_____

Where do see people most misuse the meanings of word?

_____

_____

_____

Think of a smart solution you came up with?

_____

_____

_____

ABOUT THE AUTHORS

Alex and Richa join their experiences and lessons told to their daughter Sita into a collection of short stories. Sita has been an inspiration for the stories and a great guiding light in creating them. Richa and Alex witnessed people with similar challenges whether that being in busy cities of central India where Richa grew up, or Alex's hometown in rural Appalachia, or the city in Washington DC, that shaped their stories written in this book. The stories come from volunteering, leafletting, teaching, and living life in general.

Despite growing up so far apart their lives came together at the annual Animal Rights March. Their upbringing may have been a world apart but their beliefs and ethics converge together. For Alex, Richa was the first person he had ever dated or had feelings for and naturally they got married soon after. Their shared experiences have assured them they have been bonded forever. Today they live as a happily married couple in Alexandria, Virginia with their daughter and many pets.

Editing by Jessica Powers and Wendy Simard.

Proofreading by Jessica Powers.

Design and styling by Kathy McInnis.

Design and ebook formatting by Glenn as sarco2000 on fiverr.

The artists we collaborated with on fiverr:

Helen as user gottberg for the cover

along with art for The King's Festival and The Hunt.

Ifimira for the art for Sunflower Seeds, Ant Problems,

Graduation, The Nail, Ricochet, The Mayor,

and The Bank Robber.

Mmorgan6 for the art for Stress Relief, The Pig,

Sally's Ranch, The Smart Solution, The Puppy, Sold Out,

The Town Forest, and The Dirty River.

anastasiakhm812 for the art for The Bright Kid.

alyona636363 for the art for A New Farmer.

Special thanks to our family

Rakesh and Priti Mishra, SL and Mary Sonifrank

Rohit, Ravi, and Paul

Nisha, the late Santosh Mishra, the late Ratan Mishra

Along with all our pets past and present

Kitty Beans, Okie, Miss Kitty, Gassy, Cheeba, and Miko

Made in the USA
Middletown, DE
24 August 2022

72106096R00046